The St. Rose Ghost

*Patty Cornell and Joann Benzinger with
Illustrations by Mackenzie Munie*

This book contains real characters and stories about the Ghost that lurks the halls of St. Rose School. There are also fictional additions that make the stories more interesting. It is up to the reader to decide what is real and what is make-believe.

St. Rose School District 14-15
18004 St. Rose Road
St. Rose, IL 62230
www.strosedistrict 14-15.com

authorHOUSE

AuthorHouse™
1663 Liberty Drive
Bloomington, IN 47403
www.authorhouse.com
Phone: 1 (800) 839-8640

© 2016 Patty Cornell; Joann Benzinger. All rights reserved.

No part of this book may be reproduced, stored in
a retrieval system, or transmitted by any means
without the written permission of the author.

Published by AuthorHouse 08/23/2016

ISBN: 978-1-5246-2580-1 (sc)
ISBN: 978-1-5246-2579-5 (e)

Library of Congress Control Number: 2016913798

Print information available on the last page.

Any people depicted in stock imagery provided by Thinkstock are
models, and such images are being used for illustrative purposes only.
Certain stock imagery © Thinkstock.

This book is printed on acid-free paper.

Because of the dynamic nature of the Internet, any web
addresses or links contained in this book may have changed
since publication and may no longer be valid. The views
expressed in this work are solely those of the author and do
not necessarily reflect the views of the publisher, and the
publisher hereby disclaims any responsibility for them.

This book is for the families of St. Rose School District 14-15 in St. Rose, Illinois. Small rural communities are searching for innovative ways to raise the money needed to continue the excellent education being offered to their children. *The St. Rose Ghost* was written as a fundraiser. When the going gets tough, the tough get going! Our parents are the best support system any school could ask for. This book is for them.

You are HERE!

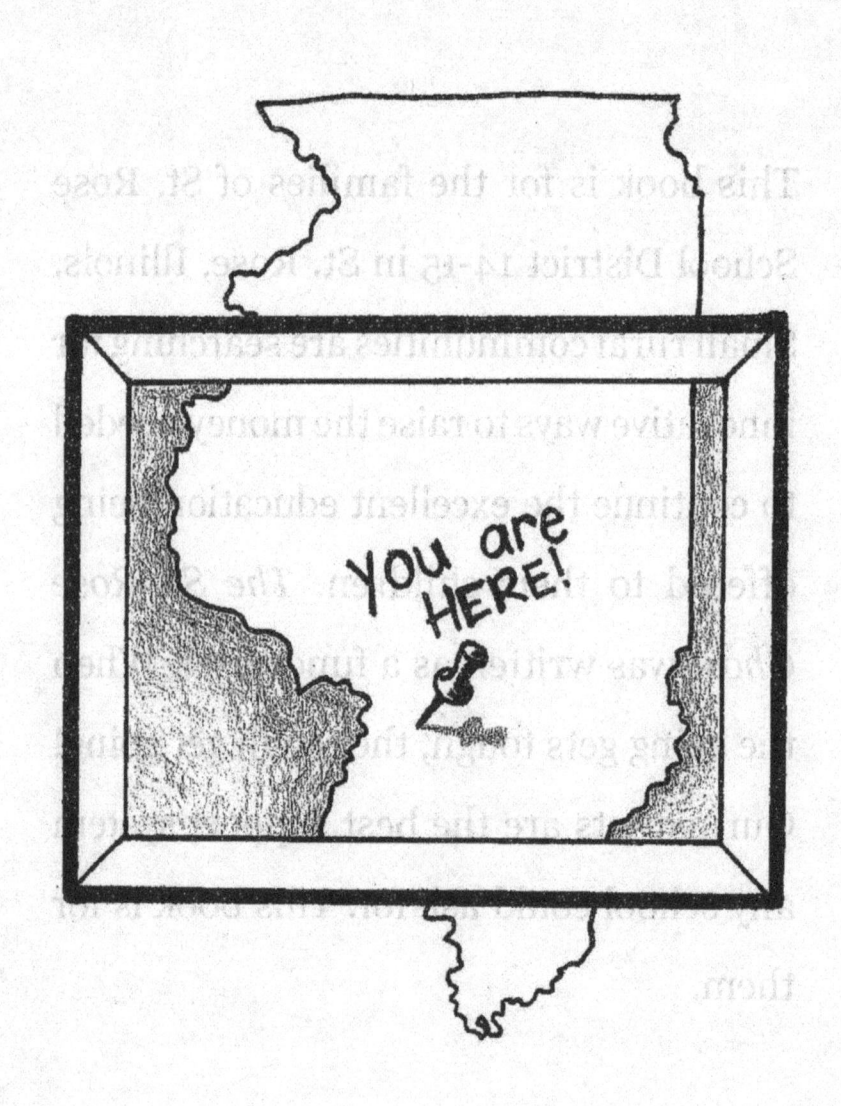

Introduction

St. Rose is a small, rural school located in south-central Illinois, but it could just as easily be a small school located anywhere in the farmlands of America. It could be the school across the street, across the state, or across the country. It doesn't matter where the school is located because this story is about people, from both the present and the past.

I've been the superintendent at St. Rose for the past nine years. During that time, I've heard many stories, many rumors, and much local lore about a ghost lurking the halls of our school. These pages are a written account of the stories relayed to me about the activities and pranks of the ghost in St. Rose School. Are they true? Is our ghost real? Or is it the product of overactive imaginations? I'll leave that decision to you. Read on, and draw your own conclusions.

The St. Rose Ghost

Rose was St. Rose's bookkeeper for more than thirty years, which makes her an honorary historian of sorts. During her time here, ghost stories swirled around her and throughout the school, but being a bit of a skeptic, she never quite believed that there was anything to it. She jokingly shared with me that the ghost was a former superintendent who was here for only a short time. The ghost stories began when he mysteriously left and died a few years later. No one really knew why he left or why he died. He just did, and to Rose's practical way of thinking, that was that.

Rose had heard knocking on the walls and water running in the bathrooms. She'd heard random toilets flushing and the inexplicable sound of footsteps, but she could always find a logical explanation, especially since the custodian had quite a sense of humor. She was a sensible woman and wasn't about to believe some nonsense about a ghost haunting the halls. However, these were enticing stories, and the more she talked, the more it piqued my curiosity!

Susi, the school board president and former bookkeeper (before Rose), also reported hearing sounds that made her think the ghost might be real: someone breathing, a low, soft howling like wind softly rustling through the trees, toilets flushing, and a louder sound like rushing water.

Occasionally, when she was working alone in the office, the sound of a door mysteriously opening and suddenly slamming shut would scare her silly. I remember once after a board meeting that ran late into the night, we stood in the halls discussing the haunting of our school. As we listened to moans and groans that are quite typical of an aging building settling in for the night, we both became aware of the eerie feeling that we weren't alone! A strange presence made the hair on our arms stand up. Needless to say, we quickly left for home.

After that experience, I asked some of the younger students for their best ghost stories. They did a wonderful job sharing. One student told me that the ghost of St. Rose was an old man who followed him around the school. He claimed that the ghost sometimes helped him do good things but at other times encouraged him to misbehave. Since this particular child was a little bit mischievous himself, I asked what exactly the ghost had led him to do. His story is as follows. (And please, don't try this at school.)

When I was in kindergarten, a ghostly old voice told me to sneak out of the classroom and go home. It was a nice day, and being outside felt better than being in school. I told the teacher I was going to the restroom, but instead, I slipped out of the building. No one saw me or heard me, so I decided to walk along the path the bus took home. I walked past the church, where Sister Justina was outside picking up pecans. She didn't see me, so I kept walking. I walked past the house with the big porch on the corner. There was a dog on the porch napping in the sun. He raised his head when I went by and gave a muffled woof. I knew he saw me, but I kept on walking.

I walked past a field where a farmer was working. He was driving a big green-and-yellow tractor but didn't see me, so I kept walking. I walked past another field where a farmer had his head thrust under the hood of his truck. He was whistling as he used a big wrench to loosen something. He dropped the wrench and stopped whistling. I couldn't hear what he said, but he didn't see me, so I just kept walking.

It felt like I had walked for a really long time. I guessed the bus didn't usually take the shortest path possible when it took me home. I started getting lonely for my friends and just a little bit thirsty.

I walked by some horses and thought about riding one back to school. I heard the ghost's raspy whisper tell me, "Go ahead and try it." I eyed a horse that looked particularly spunky. He returned my stare. He swished a buzzing fly with his tail, tossed his head, and nickered as if to say, "Go ahead. I dare you." He stared at me some more. I returned his stare. Then, bucking and kicking, the horse ran off to the opposite end of the pasture. I was glad I hadn't climbed on!

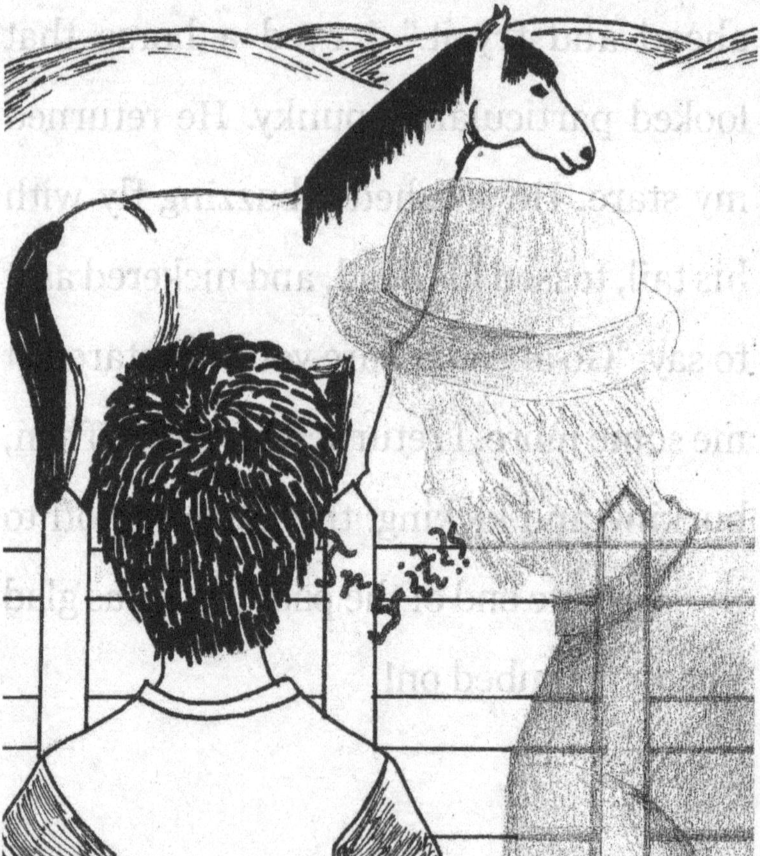

The ghostly voice croaked, "The horse was probably afraid of you anyway."

I kept walking and soon found myself by a cornfield that seemed like a good shortcut between my house and the school. The bus didn't go this way, but the throaty rasp enticed me to try it anyway. Surely the straight rows would be easy to follow to the other side. With insistence, the voice declared, "A smart boy like you knows the shortest path is a straight line through the middle of the corn." But I thought it took an awfully long time for the bus to get past the corn and decided it probably wouldn't be short enough to get me home before the end of the day.

The old man grumbled, "The corn is probably hot without the wind anyway."

I started walking again. I walked past some silos. I could see the church steeple in the distance, so I aimed for it. I walked past the farmer who had dropped the wrench; the hood on the truck was closed, and he was whistling again. His wife stood next to him holding a big glass of ice-cold lemonade. The glass was dripping with condensation, and it looked so good. I really wished I could have a drink. They didn't see me, so I kept walking.

I walked past the farmer on the green-and-yellow tractor. He didn't see me, so I

The St. Rose Ghost

kept on walking. I walked past the dog on the porch. He gave a little yip as I passed but didn't come off the porch. So I kept on walking.

I walked past the church. Sister Justina must have finished by the pecan tree, because she wasn't outside anymore, so I kept walking and soon found myself next to the drainage ditch behind the school. It looked like a safe place to hide until the end of the day when the bus would take me home. From there, I could see the school and watch for dismissal.

I'd been walking for a very long time and was getting sleepy. The coaxing of the gravelly old voice said that sleeping in the ditch would keep me safe. A nap sure sounded good! I thought about my teacher and the other kids in my class. I missed them! They wouldn't be lying in a ditch right now, trying to find a comfortable place for their heads. They wouldn't be sweaty from the long walk in the sun. They wouldn't be so thirsty their voices cracked like the voice of an old ghost. And they certainly wouldn't be trying to shift the rocks in a ditch so the sharp edges didn't poke them in the ribs. They were lying on their soft towels, listening to the soothing strains of quiet music that the teacher played every day after lunch. I thought of PE class and the games I would miss if I stayed outside.

Reluctantly, the encouraging voice agreed that I could go back to school if that was what I really wanted. So I didn't keep walking. Instead, I ran like the wind back to the front door, just as the mail person was delivering a heavy basket of mail to the office. As the door slid open, I slipped in and returned to class.

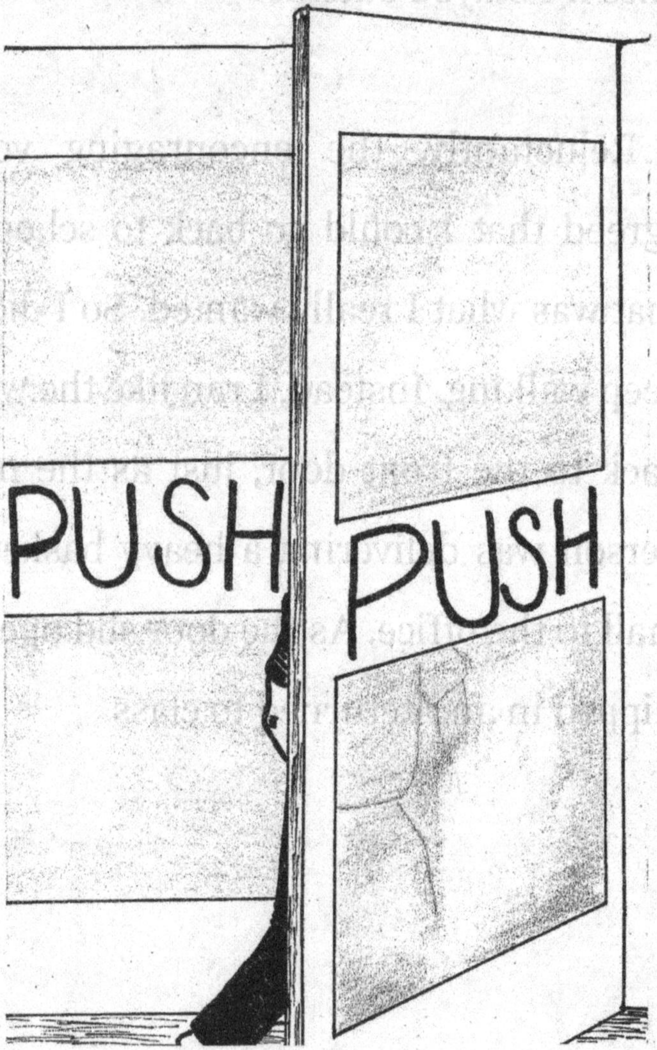
PUSH
PUSH

The St. Rose Ghost

I guess I missed nap time, because they were getting up and getting ready for gym class. I walked right in as though I'd only been gone a few minutes. It seemed funny that the teacher didn't ask me why I'd been gone so long. Didn't she realize I'd missed nap time?

The weary old man sighed and agreed that I had done the right thing by going back to school.

The little boy continued his story of our ghost. He said that another time, the ghost told him to play a trick on the custodian, Charlie. Everyone loves Charlie because he keeps the building safe and everyone healthy by keeping things clean. Here is what the boy had to say about that day:

One day I saw Charlie working on a project. He was carrying a hammer, nails, and glue up and down the stairs. Unable to resist the ghost's urging, I carried the tools to the top of the steps when Charlie wasn't looking. Poor Charlie stood there and scratched his head, wondering if he'd gone crazy. Hadn't he just carted those tools down the stairs?

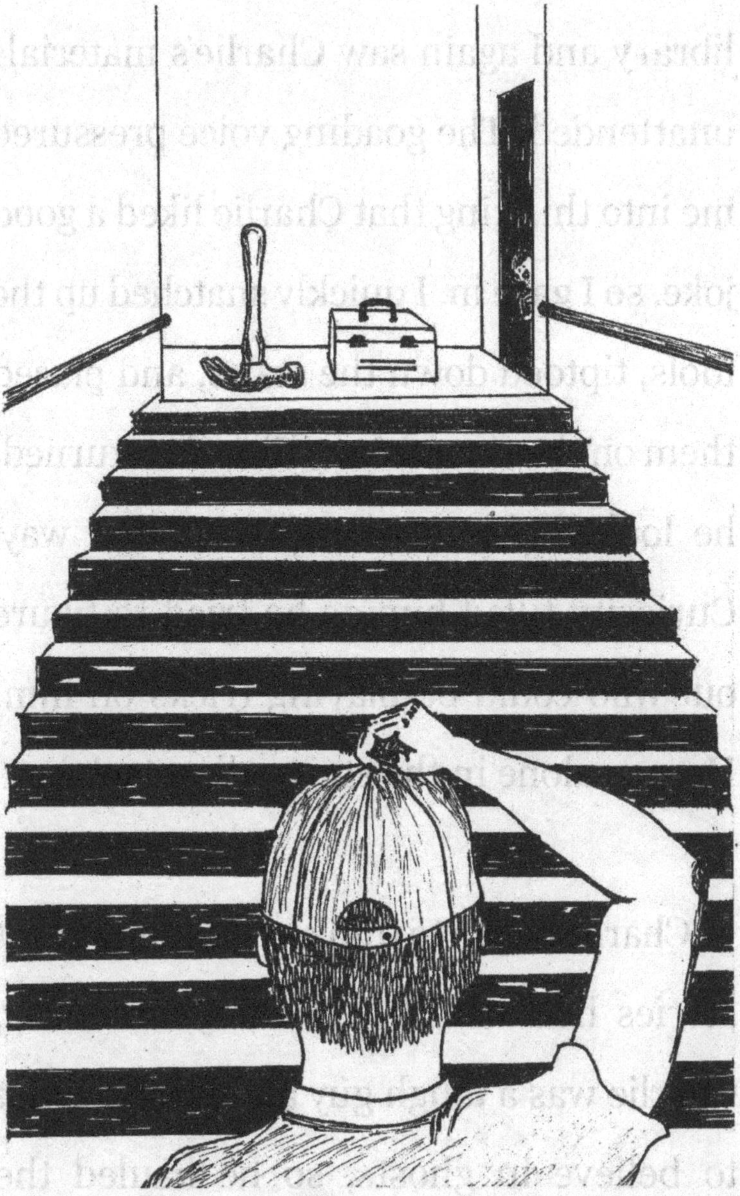

A little later, I went down to the library and again saw Charlie's materials unattended. The goading voice pressured me into thinking that Charlie liked a good joke, so I gave in. I quickly snatched up the tools, tiptoed down the stairs, and placed them on the floor. When Charlie returned, he looked this way and then that way. Curiosity filled him as he tried to figure out who could be playing tricks on him. He was alone in the stairwell, wasn't he?

Charlie began to think of the many ghost stories he'd heard over the years. Now, Charlie was a tough guy and wasn't about to believe in ghosts, so he hauled the hammer, nails, and glue back up the stairs.

As I came back from the library, I quietly picked up the hammer and concealed it under my books. Back in the classroom, I hid it in my desk and later returned for the glue. It sure was funny to see a bewildered Charlie return to find his tools missing again. I could see that he was determined to find out who was playing tricks. Later, I returned the hammer and glue. Imagine old Charlie's surprise when they reappeared just as mysteriously as they had disappeared! The old man's voice told me that giving them back was the right thing to do.

The boy continued, telling of tricks he and the ghost had played on teachers by moving their dry-erase markers around the room. He told of getting other children into trouble by dropping their pencils or making papers fly off their desk. He chuckled as he told of moving the curser around on the fourth-grade SMART Board while all the children watched in awe. His eyes were wide as he imitated the faces of the fifth-graders when he told of the mysteriously closing door when they had a guest speaker.

The little boy giggled as he told me of all the things the ghost had influenced him to do. He was entertaining, to say the least, and his stories got me wondering. I thought I'd move on and find some other stories to share and sent the boy back to class.

An older child told me that he too had heard an older voice telling him to play tricks on teachers. He laughed as he shared his story.

One day at recess, we collected seventeen grasshoppers and let them go in the classroom when the teacher was out for the day. We watched as they hopped around the room, leaping from windowsill to floor, from floor to chair, and from chair to desk. Eventually several of them made their way to the podium, where the unsuspecting substitute stood lecturing about the Civil War, proudly proclaiming something about fourscore and seven years ago. But we weren't listening; our attention was glued to the little green bug preparing to land right where she was standing. We all tried to conceal our snickering.

And then it happened. Not one but two green, long-legged grasshoppers soared through the air and landed right on the book she was reading from.

chiIIIRRKKK!

The big-eyed, juice-spitting creatures chirped their alien greeting, but we couldn't hear them over the screams of the unfortunate substitute. She raced from the room, loudly proclaiming, "Never again!" and that was the last we saw of her.

The teacher wasn't happy the next day when he came back and couldn't figure out how that many bugs got into the room.

Then I talked with a little girl who was eager to share her stories. She said the ghost could take the appearance of anyone and enjoyed playing tricks in the bathroom mirrors making the other girls scream. Legend has it that once the ghost had made a girl's hair fly all over just after she had painstakingly combed it into place. The little girl giggled with impish delight as she mimicked the face of the girl, whipping her hair around.

The little girl also told of the pranks in the kitchen. Tiffany is the school's head cook. She's a no-nonsense sort of gal and tough to convince of anything that crossed the threshold of normal. Once, the ghost turned off her ovens, leaving the children eating an emergency meal of fried chicken brought in from the restaurant across the street. The children thought it was a great adventure; the kitchen staff, however, were left baffled and a bit frustrated by the unexpected menu change. Luckily, the lasagna was just as good the next day when the ovens were working again.

The girl also shared that the lid on the garbage disposal would mysteriously shift on occasion so that when it was switched on, sludge water and chunks of debris would fly up onto the walls and ceiling, assaulting any person daring enough to have turned it on. She laughed with fiendish glee as she told of an incident involving Taco Tuesday and the lady principal. The assistant cook swore she'd had the disposal lid firmly in place as they all worked together to wipe salsa from the walls, trying hard not to laugh at the bits of tomato and onion clinging to the principal's very proper clothes.

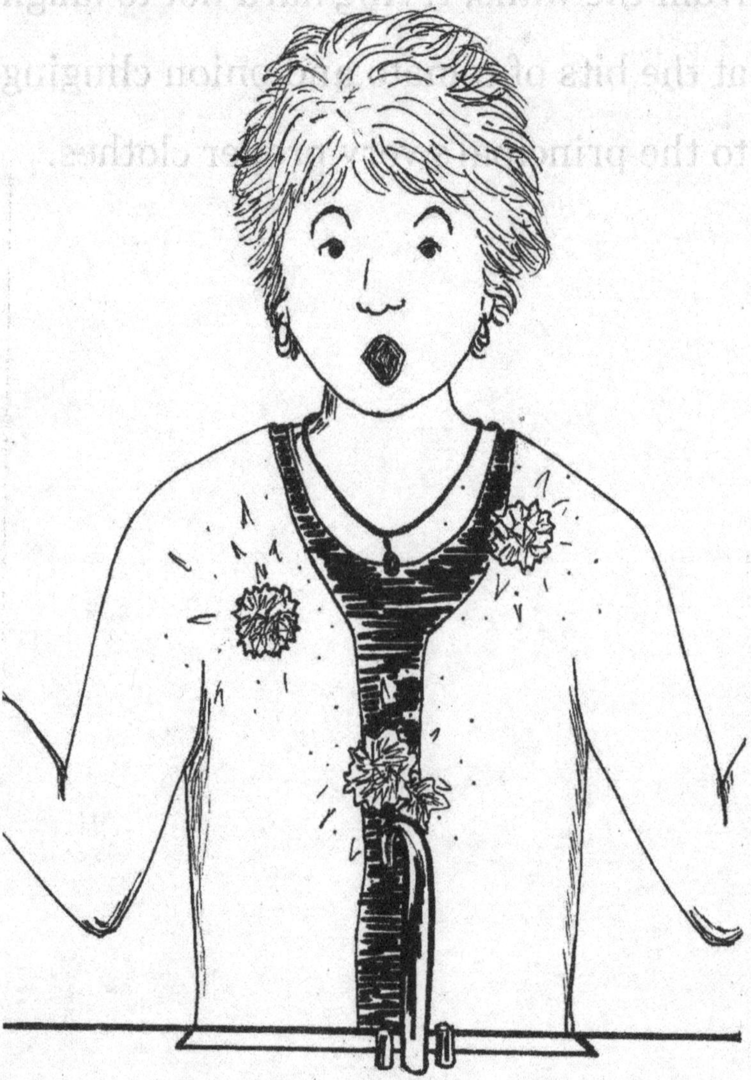

The St. Rose Ghost

According to the young girl, the basketball coach believed in the mysterious presence, claiming that the ghost made all their team's shots go into the hoop. The little girl didn't believe that one at all because no self-respecting ghost with a busy haunting schedule would spend that much time in any one place. She said that at times, though, basketballs could be heard bouncing in the gym when no one was down there.

All of these stories seemed so typical for any school and unlikely to be the activities of a ghost. I pondered all of these tidbits as I walked back toward the office through the darkened halls. Then suddenly I heard a *thump! thump!* I stopped and listened, wondering what was making that sound. Then I heard it again. *Thump! Thump!*

I cautiously asked myself, "Are those basketballs? Who could be in the gym at this hour?"

I went to check on the noise to see who had come into the building. It was already dark, and I was ready to go home. I heard the laughter of the same little boy I had talked to earlier. Now I wondered how he had gotten in and why he wasn't at home at this time of night.

The St. Rose Ghost

Then I heard it more clearly: *Thump, thump, thump! Swooooosh!*

"Who's there?" I called.

There was no answer, and I was really hoping that it was just water in the old pipes of the school or someone's lost homework paper caught in an air vent.

Then came a *stomp! stomp! stomp!* It sounded like footsteps.

I shouted a greeting: "Hello? Is anyone here?"

33

As I approached the cafeteria and crossed the hall to the gym, I heard the footsteps coming up behind me. I turned quickly to see who was there and found no one.

I continued on and again heard steps coming quickly closer. *Stomp! Stomp! Stomp! Stomp!* The faster I walked, the louder the footsteps became. Faster and faster, louder and louder, until finally the footsteps sounded like they were running, so I took off running too. The footsteps kept coming and were still getting louder and louder. Now I was sure I could hear childlike laughter, and not just one voice but two, maybe more! How could there be children in the deserted halls of the school?

Just as I reached the office and took out my keys, I heard the giggling voices of many children.

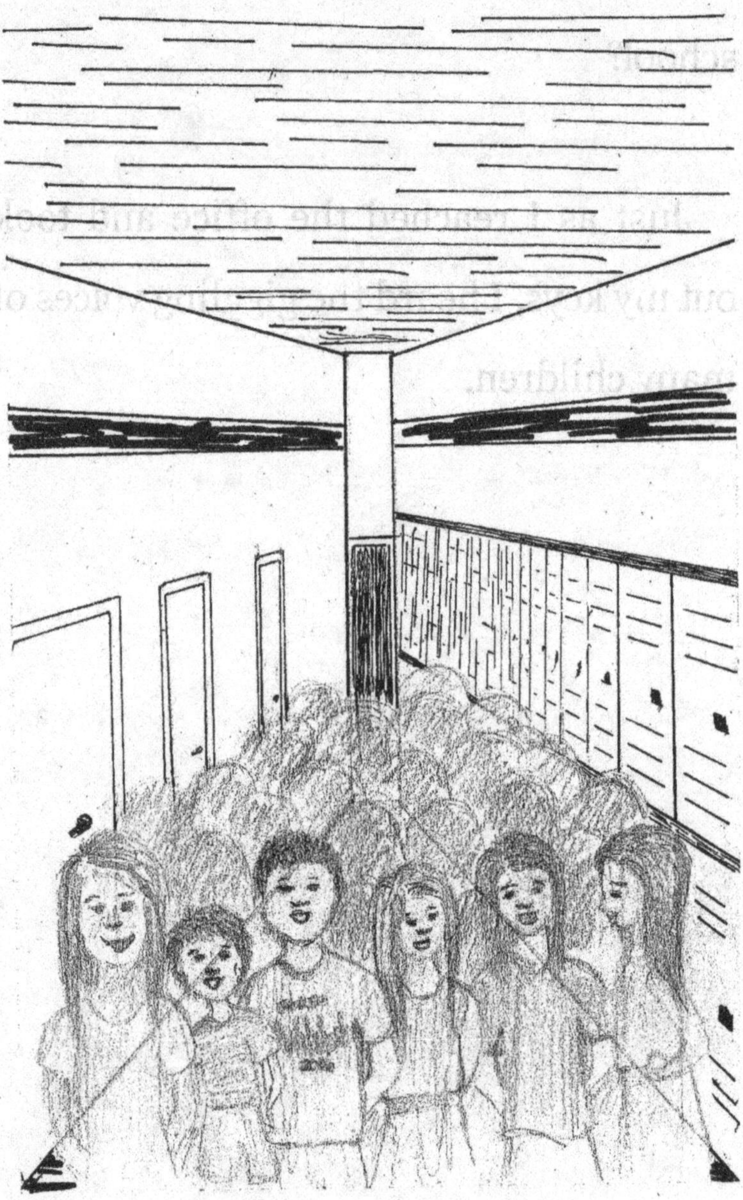

I looked up at the laughter and saw them. Imagine that. There in the hall were the shadowy figures of the two boys and girl who had told me these stories, and behind them were many more. I stared at them as they stood there giggling and clapping their hands like we were at the conclusion of some fantastically played practical joke. And then their laughter grew quieter, like they were more distant than just down the hall. The noise faded to a quiet hush. I blinked, and when I looked again, all was quiet. I was once again alone in the halls of St. Rose School.

These are the stories related to me about the activities and pranks of the ghost in St.

Rose School. Are they true? Is our ghost real? Or is it the product of overactive imaginations? Either way, the spirit of St. Rose will always live on through our "ghost." Or is it the ghost of St. Rose will always live on through our spirit? As for me, I believe.